Memoirs of
THE
PetSitteR ™

A JOURNEY WITH THE
OTHER CREATURES OF OUR LIVES   by Suzanne

TABLE OF CONTENTS

FOREWORD

My desire to write this book, Memoirs Of The PetSitteR, came to me one afternoon, after I had spent a number of hours perusing through a stack of almost two decades worth of pet sitting notes. Every time I visited a client's home, I would leave a note detailing such things as the interaction that occurred between their animal(s), critter(s) or kid(s), as I sometimes jokingly call them, and myself, along with any information concerning the health and well-being of their companion animal(s). If needed, I noted information about their home. I also jotted thoughts, what I refer to as philosophical ponderings I had while spending many quiet moments in the company of their beloved companion(s). I asked clients to please return the notes to me when they finished reading them. This was an unconscious request in regards to thinking about using the notes for a book however, here it is.

For too many years I wandered. I lost my true sense of self. And without a sense of self, I was not a contented soul. Becoming a pet sitter, The PetSitteR, helped me return to the person known as Suzanne, the person who I was born to be.

Even though I took classes such as animal behavior and nutrition, as side classes to my course of study in college, the job itself, working with and about the other creatures made me delve in to the various behavioral sciences, so that I could better understand and interact with them. Frankly, I realized this informal educa-tional process should also be applied to myself. I became my own un-P.H.d. therapist. With thoughts from collected notes and self-analysis, I have re-discovered who I actually am, from the inside, out.

My hope is that I convey my thoughts within the text in a clear, concise manner. I feel I write more eloquently than I speak. The same applies somewhat to the comic strips. However, do beware and be aware. As I have written in notes to clients, "Sometimes a mind is a terrible thing to use." Some of the comic strips do convey events that actually happened to me, or between me and/or an animal(s). Some strips contain a bit of embellishment with what actually happened, and some strips are what I call just plain stupid thinking on my behalf. I leave this to the discerning mind of the reader to decide what events may or may not be real, embellished a bit, or fictional.

There may very well be hidden or subliminal messages contained within a number of the strips. Words, wording, and/or drawings may have been manipulated to challenge the conscious mind. Once again, I leave this to the reader to discover. In some strips, I show my political, environmental, social, or soulful self by expressing my opinion on what I feel are vitally important issues. Humor is the chosen form of oration for the politician within me, and it is my coping mechanism for the difficulties that occur within daily living.

I created this book for myself, my clients, and for you. I also created it for the other creatures.
As much as possible,

"Enjoy living."

And enrich your enjoyment, by embracing the other creatures and their lives,
whether inside or outside your home.

DEDICATION

This book is dedicated to...

My Aunt Sister, Anna Claire, who taught me that I may not always understand, that at times, I just have to accept.

And to my Mother, who said,
        "Never pick a flower. Let it grow in its natural environment"
        "Never take a gemstone. Leave it to its natural setting"
        "Never cage any creature. All deserve to be free."

ACKNOWLEDGEMENTS

As I wrote in the foreword, this book came about from a request to my clients for the return of the notes I had written. What I did not realize at the time, is that a consciousness was indeed at work, a consciousness that eventually presents its-self to the mind. It comes from the Force of the ever-expanding Universe, the Force some refer to as God. It brings together... that which is meant to be. At this present moment; Me, my clients, their companion animal(s), and John.

I need to thank my clients for entrusting me with the care of their homes, their places of privacy and most important, the care of their beloved companion animal(s). It has become more than just a job.

And as for The PetSitteR comic strip, it would have never come to fruition if it depended on my right hand drawing ability. For I can draw nothing other than rough looking stick figures. No meat, no potato. A good decade or so ago, I met John McNees. We temporarily worked at a sort of resort. John was sitting outside the kitchen area with a pad of paper and pen, doodling. Just a dude doodling. I walked up to him and asked him to draw something funny. He drew a caricature of himself and that was that. I thought anyone who could and would make fun of himself was what I was looking for in an artist. John accepted the mission I put forth to him, my idea for a comic strip to accompany a book I wanted to write. He would not only have to put-up with me in general but try to draw the sometimes questionable vision of strip ideas that my mind produced, a definite paradigm shift from the traditional comic strip.

A decade of living; our jobs, the death of our Mothers, other personal happenings, along with two revisions of the current one hundred plus strips occurred, yet we persevered. John's commitment to The PetSitteR is as great as mine. This is not only my acknowledgement of appreciation to John for working with me on this project, but my thank you to him.

THE PETSITTER ™

IT'S GAME TIME

Today we're playing

―――――

"PLACES & FACES"

―――――

When taking care of the other creatures, the PetSitteR's travels take her to many different places.
Your goal is to match the appropriate face of the PetSitteR with the place she is visiting.

GOOD LUCK

―――――

THE PLACES

A HEAVENLY ACRES

B SPOOKY MANOR

C CHATEAU ON THE MARSH

THE FACES

1

2

3

How Did You Do?

ANSWERS

A - 2   B - 3   C - 1

Faces & Places

VII

© 2007 SUZ

The Illustrator

My First...

People embrace their pets as family members and, in general, many people are fascinated by them. The family pet, companion animal, is always a subject of conversation whether visiting in a home or out and about the town. The subject matter is, as the saying goes, "Near and dear to many people's heart." And conversations may include the sometimes tall tale about an encounter with a wild creature, such as, "I swear that Great Horned Owl was four feet tall."

I will never forget the first animal I could call my own. The year was 1963. I was seven years old. My friend Mary, who was also seven, and I had walked to the church on the corner located just one house away from mine. We were walking through the church parking lot when we spotted two adorable kittens. One kitten was gray and the other kitten was white. They were perhaps, seven weeks old, just two little precious lives. We took them to my house and placed them in the garage, giving them a small bowl of milk to drink.

We were standing just outside the garage, so excited, watching our two little finds, when two women who were walking in stride, side by side, turned in to the driveway and headed straight toward us. My awe and amazement toward these two women heightened as they got closer and closer to us, for you must understand that as a child, I had never seen adult twins before, at least not in person. Plus, when I was born, my right eye turned severely toward my nose bridge. Although my parents were diligent early on in making corrections to my vision impairment, I had to check my eye sight. Was that lazy eye fooling me or was I truly seeing two identical, yet separate people?

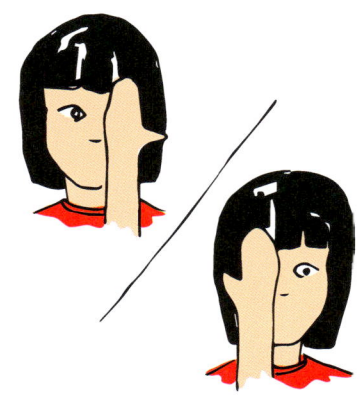

They not only looked identical to one another, their hair flipped outward in a curl just above their shoulders, their friendly-looking faces enhanced even more by the bright red lipstick that they wore, they also were dressed exactly alike. I recall that they had on white blouses and wool skirts consisting of mixes of browns in a plaid design. Over their blouses they wore dark brown colored wool coats.

Mary and I stood there paralyzed, as the sisters approached us. They spoke to us in such a kind manner, asking if we had found two kittens. We told them we had, that the kittens were in the garage, and that we had given them some milk. Well..., the sisters looked at each other, whispered back and forth to one another for a bit of time and then with a smile, one of them said, "If you promise to give the kittens a good home, take good care of them, you may keep the kittens." I remember filling with such joy. My heart seemed to open and swallow those two little punkins.

When our parents confirmed that we could keep the kittens, the sisters in stride, side by side, walked down the driveway, turned toward the church, and we never saw them again. Mary took the gray kitten home and I took the white one in to my house. I named her Snowflake. Snowflake became a parent to Snowball and a grandparent and a great grandparent.

It has been some fifty years since Snowflake entered my life, filling me with joy and wonderment. In caring for her and her descendants, I developed a sense of responsibility and respect for another creature. We bonded through trust. We became a pack of companions. I loved them.

Even to this day, when I think about them, I miss those kitties. A thought I wrote a number of years ago and maintain to this day in keeping cherished remembrances, such as those two little kittens, is

"When remembering loved ones,
whether human or animal,
miles and memories,
not so distant
when thought of through the heart."

PetSitteR 101

KiTTens

Can be...

Screamin' Mimis

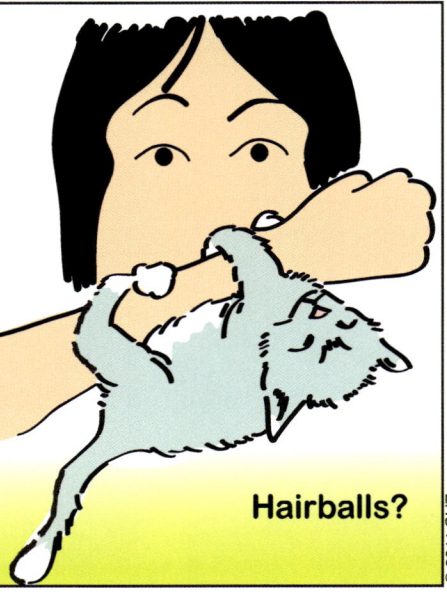

Hairballs?

Tree huggers?

Kittens Can Be

After you.

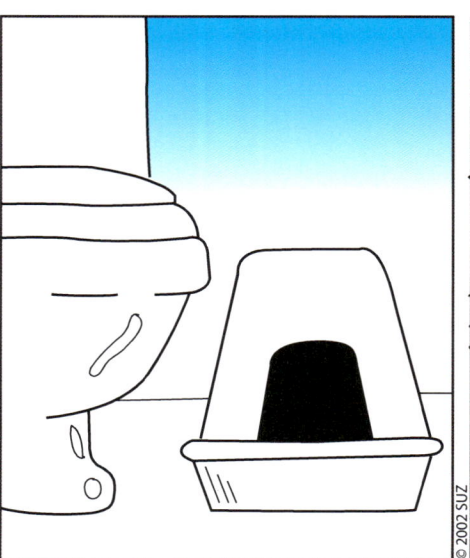

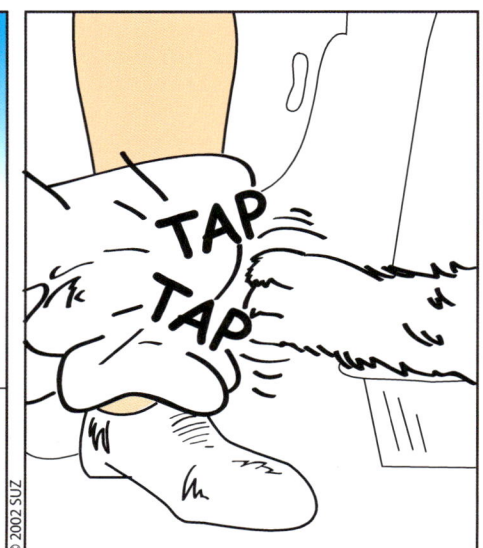

TAP
TAP

Cat Toiletpaper

The Me...

I have never given much thought to getting married and/or having children. I did receive several marriage proposals but... . And I did pursue a number of relationships but... . So many, many years ago, when people inquired about my conjugal state, in jest I told them that I was a spinster. I am a spinster. For those of you who are unsure what a spinster is, the term is defined as, a woman beyond the marrying age of thirty, childless. And yes, to expand on the definition I currently have one cat. However, I am not just a woman who happens to be a spinster, I am an amalgamation of many personas.

During the time that my body was changing from that of the care-free little girl to a young woman, my Mother introduced me to make-up. For a brief period of time I wore the tan colored tone of base. And yes, I learned to rub it in under the jaw line, so that there would not be a demarcation between tan face and white neck. Lipstick did not appeal to me, nor did eye make-up, so I never wore either of these. My Mother definitely liked to wear lipstick and she wore eye make-up, although modestly applied. She was confident in who she was and she felt that this confidence was most evident when portrayed through as natural of a self as possible.

The influence of my Mother for me to maintain the natural self, coincided with the personae I had of myself as that of a literally, young hippie in regards to the Drug, Sex, and Rock n' Roll era of the mid to late Sixties. For me, being a hippie meant to step out of society's construct of who I should be as not only a person but as the female. It was the ultimate paradigm shift; freedom, expression, experimentation, open-ended. Unknown to me at the time, I was constructing the person I was born to be. I was fashioning me from the inside out.

There was however, at least one time, if not two, when the me was externally decorated. I was asked to participate in one of my cousin's matrimonial celebrations and in my youngest brother's wedding. From head to toe I looked spanky, uncomfortable, but spanky in a dress, nylons, and footwear other than tennis shoes or flip flops, and of course, make-up. I do believe my eyes were finally introduced to and highlighted with a bit of mascara, and whatever it is that is applied above the eye and below the eyebrow. My lips had stick on them, and my nails, fingers and toes, had polish applied to them. Now my color of choice for lips and nails would have been that of a Madame Red, but it was not my day of celebration, so... . And least I forget to mention that in one of the weddings, someone got-a-hold-of my hair. Lord help me, that stick-em stuff was sprayed in my hair to keep it in a fluffed type bun thing on top of my head.

As the girl who advanced in to a young woman during the sixties, I had unconsciously used a metaphor to express my feeling about the non-importance of the physical in comparison to the development of the emotional and spiritual self. I would say to people that my hair was born free, and it was going to stay free. Nowadays I say that my hair will forever stay long, unfettered by the bun, and as it grays, even though a few bald spots may develop here and there, I will not care. Perhaps in my elder years, just for the fun of it, I will wear base again, and purposefully leave a distinguishable line between my face and neck. Too, why not ruby-up my lips.

Stand in front of the mirror.
Look beyond the physical.
Search for your true... self.

"The magic of a mirror,
looking-out, into your self."

9

THE PETSITTER™

Until I can think of a way ...

to mend Pandy's broken heart ...

certain measures have been taken.

Garfield & Me

Pandy, when I was much younger, I was introduced to many fictional characters.

And you know, to this day, I still believe in them …

… because they live within my heart … as does Garfield live within yours.

So, by the power of putting pen to paper, and an okay by Mr. D …

Garfield & Me

© 2008 SUZ

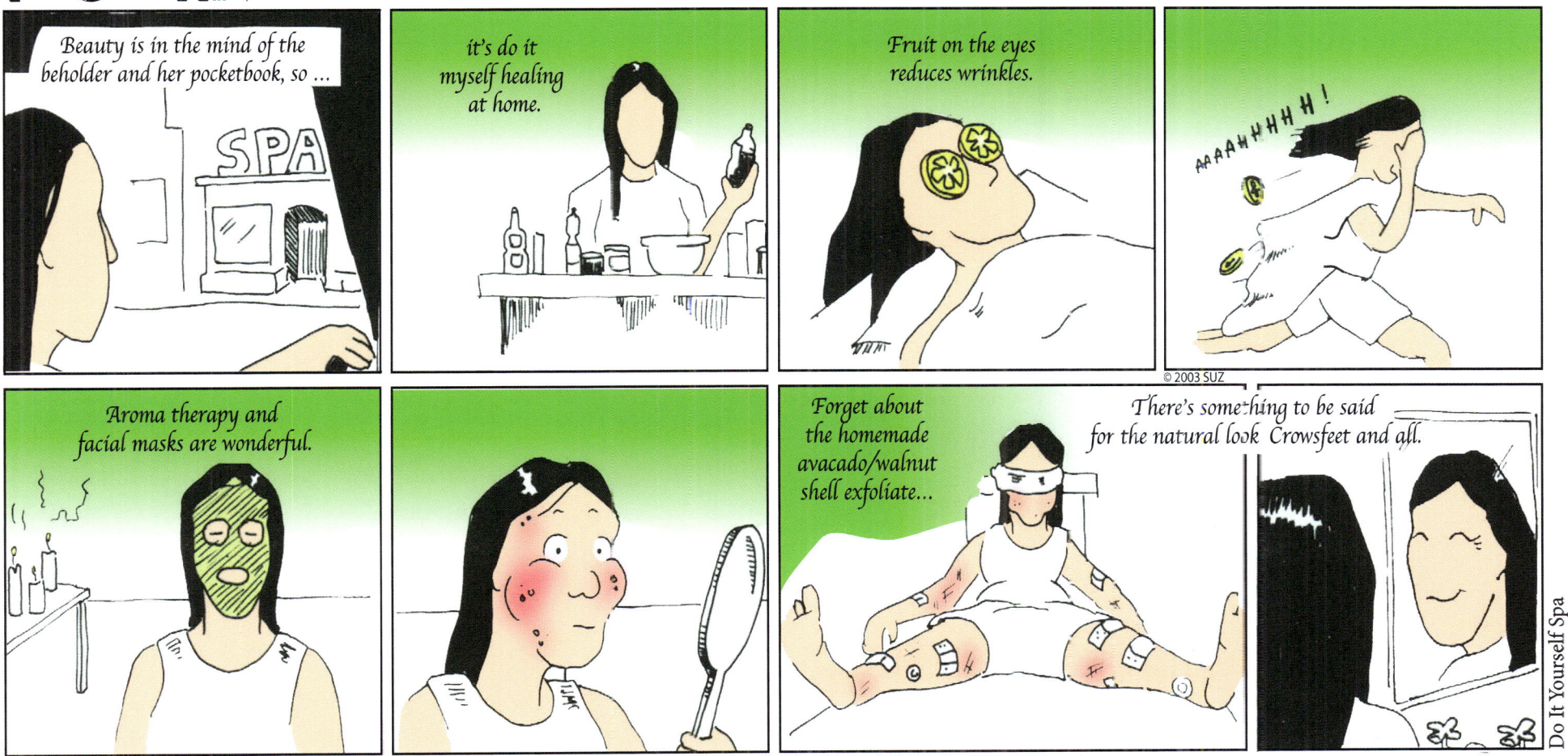

Well, Knee-Deep

Perhaps I am the old soul. I tell people I feel I could have lived comfortably in the 1800s; a self-sufficient person who lived from whatever the land produced or allowed her to produce. My life would have probably resembled that of the animals, with only the need for food, water, shelter, protection, and possibly a mate for... reproductive purposes(?).

It was during the time as a student in the seventh grade that I questioned whether or not I wanted to continue to carry a purse. I had left my purse laying on my assigned desk in a classroom and several girls decided to go through it. I returned to catch them in the act, so nothing was taken. However, I remember thinking that I did not want to have to worry about keeping my purse with me at all times for fear of this happening again. I definitely needed to carry a book bag. Did I really need a purse?

At the time, it was becoming more acceptable for females to wear slacks. I liked to wear dresses and skirts, but when the weather turned cold, I had to wear leggings under the dress or skirt to keep my bottom half warm. In thinking about the benefits of wearing slacks, I realized I could eliminate the bundled layering of clothing feeling in keeping warm. Too, many styles of slacks had pockets. Pockets hold items. So through deductive reasoning, I decided that a liberation of sorts for me was needed. I would wear slacks. And wearing slacks better fit, so to write, my tomboy personae.

I eliminated the purse from my life. No more worrying about it and its questionable, valuable contents. My house key and lunch money went in to my pants pockets. Any other personal possessions, such as a hair brush was kept in my book bag. The leggings..., my sister may have inherited these.

I do not know how and when the purse became such an integral part of women's ensemble. Initially I carried a purse because I thought that was what all girls, young women, and women did. All of the women in my life, my grandmothers, aunts, and especially my Mother carried one. And as most little girls, I wanted to emulate what my Mother did.

Even if there had not been the incident in seventh grade eventually, I believe I would have eliminated the carrying of a purse. For my Mother, it was not only the tool she used to carry her things about in, yet it was the appendage of expression in being a woman. For me it is not.

Just as I eliminated the purse, I work to either remove or to keep from acquiring more stuff in my life. It took me a bit of time to acquire a cell phone, something that became necessary because clients are letting-go of their landlines. I have not acquired cable television or internet service in my home. Temptation swirls about my head the most, in whether or not to purchase cable television. I enjoy watching the classic sitcoms and movies, food or animal related programs that I can frankly, view while staying in client homes. After the animal(s) needs are met, I can easily go into just sittin and clickin mode. I cannot monetarily justify having even the most basic plan in cable television nor internet service. Due to my chosen profession, both wants would sit idle more times than not. I have post-it notes on my bathroom mirror. One is a suggestion I once heard Suze Orman make that states, "I have more money than I will ever need." By living as simple as possible, living within my means, I feel as if my business is...a lucrative journey.

In learning to discern needs from wants, I ultimately realized,

"My needs are simple,
and my wants are few."

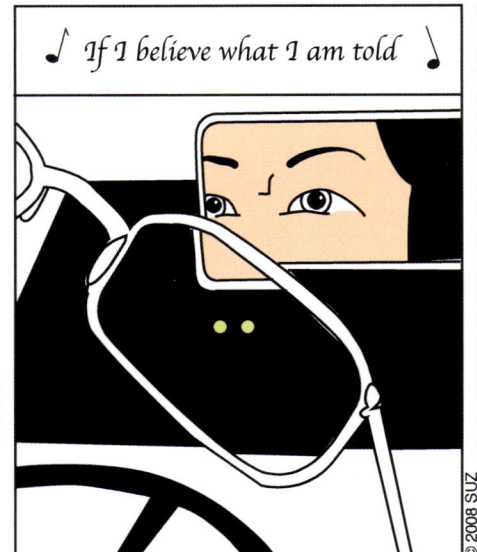

18

The PetSitter™

Illustrator's Comment

At times, the PetSitteR has asked me to draw panels that were difficult or uncomfortable for me to draw.
The third verse to this ditty fits the latter. So I took the easy way out.

This time.

JMc

♪ * Had to buy a new brassier.

Sing to the tune of "Help me make it through the night"

♪ Started saggin' just this year. ♪

♪ If I believe what I am told ... ♪

♪ It ain't easy getting old. ♪

It Ain't Easy Getting Old - Brassiere

© 2006 SUZ

The PetSitter™

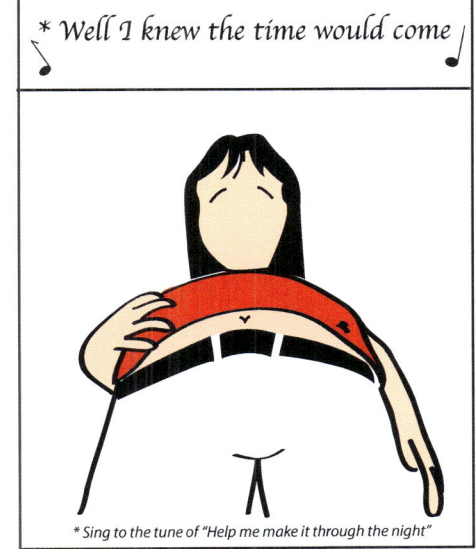

♪ * Well I knew the time would come ♪

Sing to the tune of "Help me make it through the night"

♪ when I could play my belly drum ♪

DRUM SOLO — **WIPE OUT**

♪ If I believe what I am told. It ain't easy getting old. ♪

It Ain't Easy Getting Old - Belly

© 2008 SUZ

19

♫ * Had to get down on my knees.

* Sing to the tune of "Help me make it through the night"

♫ Lord, won't you help me get up please. ♫

♩ If I believe what I am told ... ♩

♫ It ain't easy getting old. ♩

It Ain't Easy Getting Old - Knees

© 2007 SUZ

♫ * As my arches start to fall ♩

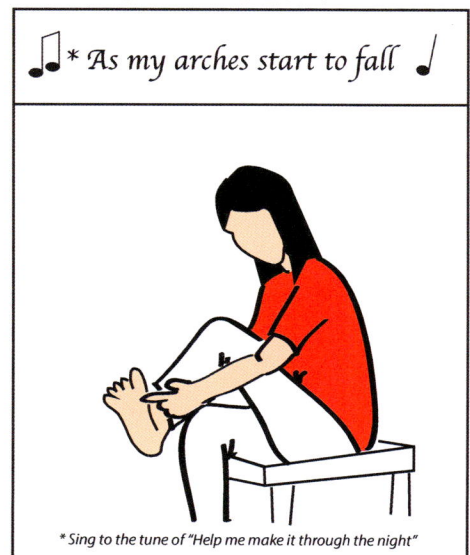

* Sing to the tune of "Help me make it through the night"

♩ I realize I'm not as tall ♩

♫ It ain't easy getting old ♩

♩ or at least that's what I'm told. ♩

It Ain't Easy Getting Old - Arches

© 2008 SUZ

♪ * My reflection shows gray hair. ♪

♪ I'm just going to leave it there. ♫

♩ It's not easy getting old ... ♫

♪ But frankly, I think it's sexy. ♩

* Sing to the tune of "Help me make it through the night"

© 2007 SUZ

It Ain't Easy Getting Old - Hair

Pandy and I like watching the classic sitcoms.

We enjoy the whistling and finger snapping theme song...

and especially, the show where vittles are mentioned in every episode.

Are we WATCHING too much television?

Pandy Classic TV

Tracer and I are hanging-out, getting ready to watch a Rugby match.

Need munchies ...

and liquid refreshment.

How uncouth.

Tracer Rugby

23

Cows in Pasture

24

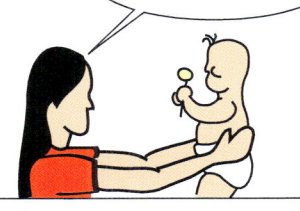

PETSITTING 101

Today's subject
Homo sapien Care

Hello little human creature.

This strip is pure folly. I, The PetSitteR, will never advocate the following methods.

A closet that has lighting works best. Remember to put newspapers on the floor.

Depending on the young'uns age, a chew toy or a book can alleviate boredom leading to mischief.

Most importantly, provide plenty of water and food. Oh, and a good lock for the closet... I mean playroom.

Homo sapien Care

© 2007 SUZ

At Issue...

In my chosen profession I work alone. All the alone time I spend with the animals is not only filled with a lot of physical activity and trying to keep-up with them, but also with what I call, constant cranial exercise. I spend countless hours thinking about many anything's and everything's. I think about things that I can consciously identify via my senses and those things that I can only try to make sense of via my pondering, such as living and its continuum, death. And I think a lot about relationships and the influences that they have on one another. I wonder about myself, the other creatures, and societies.

As a child, I loved to run through the yards in my neighborhood and bike around the church parking lot not two doors from my house. What made the church parking lot especially fun was that the pavement encircled the church, like a moat surrounding a castle. Oh-h the competitive races my friends and I would have biking around the lot. Some races were more than bike against bike. We formed teams on wheels. One child would propel a bike while another child would be seated in a wagon tied to the back of the bike. Many times while in the wagon, I hung-on for my life. It was the competition, the athletic component that thrilled us all, pushing us to do sometimes ridiculous maneuvers while trying to pass one another and going for the glory.

One time I was knocked unconscious when the wagon I was riding in took a turn too fast. Both the wagon and I went rolling. I think I was spared the wagon rolling over my head, but I was not spared my head greeting the pavement in an abrupt fashion. I vaguely remember in my groggy headed state, the trip to the doctor. Much to my parents chagrin, I was again, back in the wagon. Eventually, we moved farther down the street to a much larger home with an even bigger yard to play in, sparing my parents any future medical costs from tikes on bikes in the church parking lot. However, with the move to our new home and yard, came a field, a wonderful field just two lots from ours.

The field was like a hole dug into the earth. It was a very large area surrounded by variously sized hills that touched one another, creating the effect of a hole. There were plenty of trees, bushes, open grassed areas, and winding paths throughout its landscape. It was a virtual heaven of adventures for all of us. The field became another area for one's athletic prowess and a haven for many competitions of sorts. My brothers, sister, and I, along with new friends that we made from the move, ran, romped, and biked about the field. One of the more thrill-filled competitions that we created, was a broad jump beyond Olympic proportion. We would see who could propel him or herself out the farthest from a hilltop and fall the longest before hitting a bottom area of the field. Visits had to be made to doctor's offices, but not by me thank goodness. And if I did not want to go to the field, I stayed home and played in our yard, especially the side yard.

The side yard was as big as a football field, or at least it seemed that big to me at the time. Occasionally, my parents would have the badminton net set-up. At times, even when I played against my Mom, I would whack the birdie as far as I could. I made her run more than I should have. "Sorry Mom." And when the badminton net was put away, I waited patiently to be picked for a team during one of my older brother's organized side-yard football games. I was always chosen. I was good. I had to be good. I was the only girl who dared play with the boys. A tomboy by some, but I did not care. Many times while playing, I had to run as fast as I could, especially if I had the ball and Big Jim was chasing me. I was by no means, "a girlie girl." I never have been one to scream however, when Big Jim came after you, even some of the boys screamed.

Even though I continued to participate in the usual child-oriented physical activities around our neighborhood, I began to enjoy and greatly appreciate the athletic opportunities offered as I advanced through each grade in elementary school. During recess, I always looked forward to playing kickball. And once again, just as I would send that birdie a-flying, I would send that ball via my kick, a-sailing. One of the best opportunities for me to compete not only against my self, but other students occurred when we participated in The Presidents All American Physical Fitness Test. Actually, it was not suppose to be competitive, as much as it was suppose to help children gain fitness. I always scored well in the test.

It was during my elementary school years, I believe I was in the third grade, when the Eastwood Little League came to fruition. Through either a donation or purchase of land, my father along with a number of other community members, spent many hours creating ball fields with manicured grass outfields and dirt infields dragged to a glass like surface. They fenced and landscaped around the perimeter of the fields, graded areas for the parking lots, built wooden bleachers and a concession stand, my favorite place to visit while at the ball fields. I always purchased frozen chocolate malts with the small, novel wooden spoon.

Opening day for the baseball season was always a fun day of activities and celebration. The day began with a parade that started at the community fire station. All of the teams were dressed in their respective uniform and they walked behind their sponsor's decorated vehicle. Fire trucks and police vehicles, with sirens screaming, escorted the teams along the route to the fields. It was a walk of about eight blocks to the ball fields. People along the parade route would cheer and applaud the boys, wishing them luck in their games.

My Dad umpired games. He was acknowledged by community members and the league as someone who called a fair, impartial game and because of this, he was able to umpire some of my brother's games. I would stand at the fence near the dugout for my brother's team and cheer them to victory. And many times while I cheered for them, I wondered why I could not play. Why little girls could not, "play ball."

Junior high school gave me even greater exposure to athletics. Although track, tennis, and basketball were the only sports offered to young women, I participated in all three. One of my fondest memories is when my basketball team returned to school. We had played an away game against a tough rival and had defeated them. Our school was having a dance. Instead of hanging-out at the ping pong tables as I usually did during a school dance, I stood just inside the double doors to the gymnasium to listen to the hip songs played by the disc jockey, and watch students groove to the music.

As the disc jockey prepared to play another song, he announced our basketball team, not the boy's team, but the girl's team had won yet another basketball game. He then dedicated the song to us, Everybody is a Star by Sly and the Family Stone. The smile that came to my face was as broad and cheesy as the Cheshire Cat's. I felt such a sense of self-worth and importance. I, along with my teammates, was no longer the girl who had to stand outside the ball field fence and cheer the boys. I was on the court and I was being cheered.

I will never let go of that night nor will I forget my junior high school physical education teacher and coach, Miss Dorothy Hall. I admired her for her athletic abilities, her wisdom, and her spirit. She was always open to conversation. She listened intently and sincerely to what I had to say. And when I questioned her about the various athletic opportunities for women while she was growing-up, she freely talked about her participation in sports offered to females at that time.

During the time Miss Hall played basketball, the appropriate attire was a short sleeved shirt and a skirt. The game was played on a half court and there were six players from each team on the court. She showed me how a free throw shot was made. The player would hold the ball, one hand placed on each side of it, bend slightly at her knees, lower the ball, place it between her knees, and with an upward motion, pitch the ball toward the basket. More times than not Miss Hall proved to us, her players, that this was an easier, more accurate shooting style to use than the over the head pitch for a free throw. She also showed me a small, silver horn used prior to the introduction of the whistle, to call a gym class to order. At the time it seemed silly to hear her toot it, I guess because it was something from the past that I was unaccustomed to. Now I have that horn displayed in my bookcase, and I occasionally take it out and blow it.

My high school years fell near the end to the Civil Right's Movement and, unfortunately civil unrest. Riots even touched within the confines of my high school. I recall more than once having to leave school prior to its official days end. The principal would announce over the p.a. system that school was closing for the day and to vacate the building via a specific area. It meant a fight was taking place, a fight involving more than one individual toward another. As did many students, I would leave school in a frightened, bewildered, and sad state of mind. I did not understand why there was so much hatred of one person for another just because the other person was of a different skin color.

In junior high sports and now in high school, many of my teammates, friends, were black, colored as the term at the time was used. I do not recall any conversations between us that pertained to the difference in our skin tone. We were girls and now young women who shared a love for, and enjoyment of athletic competition. And we strove through encouragement of one another, to be the best we could be as students and as athletes.

In reminiscing, as much as physical activity has always been a part of my life, I think athletic activity in my younger years also became an escape for me, even if for just a few hours while running through the field or competing on the court, from all the insane violence that occurred during the 1960s and early 1970s. So many issues came to the forefront of our nation, issues that needed to be addressed, that tragically resulted in injuries or death to many people just because of ideological differences.

I have not directly introduced the topic to this story that also came to the forefront of our nation in the early 1970s. As a child I did not have a name for it nor did I as a young woman, at least not until I was in my second year of high school. It was 1972 when I could finally put a name to something I first alluded to when I could only stand at the fence and watch the boys play baseball, that of being treated differently because I was a girl. The ideology that perplexed me for so many years was equality, specifically equality of the sexes and, for me, equality of the sexes in athletics. Through the winning of a court case in which a challenge was made toward the inequalities in education, Title IX was created.

Title IX allegedly was the answer to many of the inequalities that had plagued our society when it came to the sexes and the treatment of women versus their male counterparts. For me it seemed a saving grace to the inequality I had felt from childhood on into adolescence in regards to one of my passions, athletics. Title IX meant equality. I remember hearing and seeing the term equality used many times. I also remember changing my thinking in the use of it to one I felt was more appropriate, equity.

I think at the time the term equality lost its relevance because it was used so often in discussions and seemed to only elicit comparisons of the sexes, amounting to nothing more than lists of differences instead of solutions and the implementation of the solutions to righting the inequalities females faced versus males. Equity made for a better challenge intellectually in the "Battle of the Sexes." It was an uncommon word. Perhaps implicit in its definition was the acknowledgment of differences between males and females. Argument also focused, as is and has to be, on budget requirements in making the required changes solicited by the implementation of this entitlement. Equalizing the benefits males received and enjoyed in athletics versus females was not the easy task.

In regards to athletics, Title IX states, "No person shall, on the basis of sex, be excluded from participation in, be denied the benefits of, be treated differently from another person or otherwise be discriminated against in any interscholastic, intercollegiate, club or intramural athletics offered by a recipient, and no recipient shall provide any such athletics separately on such basis."

Many years have come and gone since the inception of Title IX. It is a moot point and I believe it will continue to be, as to how much change leading to equality in not just athletics, but other areas such as education and employment has occurred. At a minimum, I am grateful in having Title IX as a resource if a question begs for help about one person's treatment versus another person's.

I wanted to lead you via my life's journey to the point in this country's history that ultimately would affect the course of how, specifically, athletic programs for females in schools and in communities would change, creating a more equal playing field. Title IX was, is supposed to allow for the change that gives the little girl, the young woman, and the woman such as myself the opportunities in sports, education, and the workplace as is given the little boy, young man, or man.

The issue is not about strength, endurance, power, perspiration, or dedication. I know males are physically different than me. The issue is about giving me, equity(?). It is about giving me the same opportunities on any playing field.

Out of the sixties and perhaps even earlier, women took hold of the adage, "You've Come A Long Way Baby." As does everything through the process of time, language, terms used to express current trends change. Maybe a more appropriate saying to the moot point of whether or not Title IX has been effective is,

"We're On The Move Babe."

One time during a walk, I decided May and I should do what my dad used to say, …

© 2008 SUZ

"Sometimes you just have to sit and watch the world go by."

The house is just over the hill.

Watch The World Go By

Looky thar Pandy. Ducks.

I wonder what kind they are? They're purty.

Well... "thar ducks, as you so eloquently speak, are Buffle Heads. Bucephala albeola. They are the smallest duck. However, notice their large heads.

I guess if I've seen one duck butt, I haven't seen them all.

Pandy Duck Butts

The PetSitter's challenge. Two dogs, two ways of life.

Archie and his ball to my left, Cassidy and her frisbee straight ahead.

The intersection at which a 90 degree angle meets, a balance.

I have learned the way of the Pooh-chi.

Archie & Cassidy Poo-Chi

Columbus Doorbell

Pandy The PetSitteR Crawl

PetSitteR's Tip 114

When you have two felines who aren't on the best of terms …

Belly licker.

Walking hairball.

… a simple squirt or two from a water bottle, brings the dispute to an end.

© 2001 SUZ

After that, you can fake it. Watch.

You can't hit the corner of a round box.

You came from more than one daddy.

Psssst.

Uh - OH.

Love you.

No, I love you.

You're purrfect.

No. No. You are.

Kitty Waerbottle

37

Skijoring

THE PETSITTER™

Walking with Beau and Jake, a.k.a. Stickman

can be ...

© 2001 SUZ

a real ...

TRIP

Beau & Jake The Stickman

THE PETSITTER™

Bi-ped versus Quadriped. Evolution ... P-SHAW.

© 2006 SUZ

Riley Race For The Raspberries

39

The World of Pelle and Trax

Welcome to... The World of Pelle and Trax

See ya later.

Yes folks, this actually happened.

Pelle & Trax Pet Wrestling Federation

Games Creatures Play

Your turn ...

Thank you.

Beau, Jake ... come.

I thought that was just a human thing.

Beau & Jake Spin The Turtle

THE PETSITTER™

CAT BOXES 101

TODAY'S SUBJECT: SCOOPERS

There are many tools you can use to get the job done ...

but the best one is this. It's sturdy and designed for easy handling.

Just don't get the cheap ones.

Tomorrow: Types of Litter

© 2001 SUZ

PetSitteR 101 Scoopers

THE PETSITTER™

CAT BOXES 101

TODAY'S SUBJECT: LITTER

Cats, by nature, are a clean species.

© 2001 SUZ

There are many types of fillers on the market.

Some clump ...

some deodorize ...

some need chemical reactions to work. My favorite?

No fuss, no mess.

PetSitteR 101 Litters

Spunky Dead Mice

Them...

As a country pet sitter, my work is beyond the confines of society's walls. My office setting consists of the animals I am caring for, myself, and more times than not, our existence as a part of the natural world. There are no streets with the noises of traffic flowing here and there past buildings with people coming and going. There is just the sights and sounds of farmland, forest, marsh, or prairie grassland; beautiful ecosystems flowing here and there, coming and going with, and about us.

Some of my most precious moments have been when I am alone without another human nearby. I can and I do "piddle away time" doing human things, and I thoroughly enjoy myself, my time, the moment that turns into many moments. Granted I may not be completely alone because I am usually with one or multiples of the other creature. I cannot imagine nor do I want to imagine not having them about my life. We spend time, valued by me and I hope by them, interacting with one another, yet at times, although we are within physical proximity to one another, we do our own species thing. Non threatening, separate actions of the blended pack.

For them, the animals, to allow me to be within their presence even though I look different, smell different, and questionably, act different is a privilege. I have to establish a sense within them that they can trust me by spending a period of time together in a positive, reinforcing manner. Perhaps as I know I need to respect them for who they are and what they can do, especially in regards to my safety in being with them, they too, do the same in their observations of me. After all, I can only make guesses as to how I am perceived by them; my presence and relationship to them as the worthy contributor, the possible mate, or even the challenger to their existence.

Many of the creatures that I care for are social beings just like humans. The dynamics of their natural communities of the school, flock, herd, litter, or pack are not that different from the human society in regard to needs. The difference between humans and the other creatures, is that humans have wants, a moot point in regard to the necessities to living a fully functioning and healthy life. As for relationships, there are similarities between the other creatures and humans. Some mate for life as the monogamous pair, whereas others mate via the group dynamic, a number of females to a male. Their bonds are just as close and committed, as are humans, perhaps never leaving one another until sadly, death do they part, words stated by humans in their most sacred form of commitment. And as with humans, after having reached a certain age, the young of some of the other creatures will leave their parents and/or community to create their own family/community. Too there are animals, as there are humans who for varied reasons of their nature, reside alone.

Just as we are individuals, recognized as this by our various attributes, so too are the animals. Just as we have and express emotions, sometimes to our detriment by our reactions to situations via our emotionally based response, so too do animals have emotions and they do express them. During two separate fawning seasons, some canines and I had the unfortunate pleasure of meeting an especially protective, Mama Doe. When she stomped one of her front legs, snorted, and charged after the dogs who proceeded to take flight in my direction, I decided I too, needed to leave the position I had chosen behind a tree and as they did, take flight due to fright. No fight. No further zone assessment was needed, just flight. Mama Doe was in protection mode due to her emotional attachment to her fawn(s). I have found these shared emotional responses in behavior, as evidenced by the example, to be a comfort in regard to my individualism from them. We are never alone.

I feel the relationship that develops between the animals and myself is not based upon commensalism. It is symbiotic, however I do believe that all of us benefit in a much grander form, beyond that of such basic needs as food sharing or group protection. I believe there is an eventual merging of our souls; the non-physical energy that becomes an eternal bond.

To the other creatures,

"You Never Cease to Amaze me."
Thank You.

47

Hair Whipper

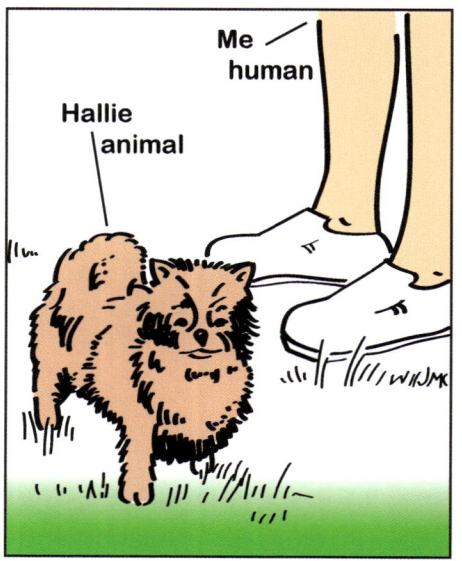

Hallie Go Low

Here's Skipper

Rusty Peeing

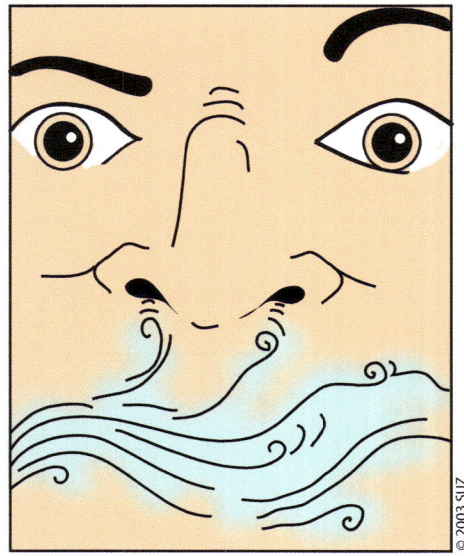

What is that refreshing odor, Chewy?

Arolin Thehay
COLOGNE
by
Chewy

What every man dog needs to please the girl dogs.

Chewy Arolin The Hay

Barn kitties need lovins' too

And that's all folks.

Mo, Daryl, Jelly, Tiger, - Kitty Lovins

50

THE PETSITTER

Mornin' kitties. Are you hungry?

WHAT THE HECK ???

© 2001 SUZ

NOT AGAIN.

STAY TOONED

Raccoon Challenge

Raccoon Challenge pt. 2

THE PETSITTER™

The Hover Dog.

I don't think her feet ever touch the ground.

Could it be those ears? Those wonderful flappable ears.

Madeline, time to go in.

© 2001 SUZ

A perfect four-point landing.

CANINE AERODYNAMICS 101

Madeline Canine Aerodynamics

53

THE PETSITTER™

Meet One-eyed Jack, the piranha

Lunchtime, Jack.

PLOP!

Ahhh… the familiar plop sound of lunch.

I must be getting old. I was sure I heard lunchtime.

One-Eyed Jack

© 2001 SUZ

THE PETSITTER™

Here you go Mr. Frog.

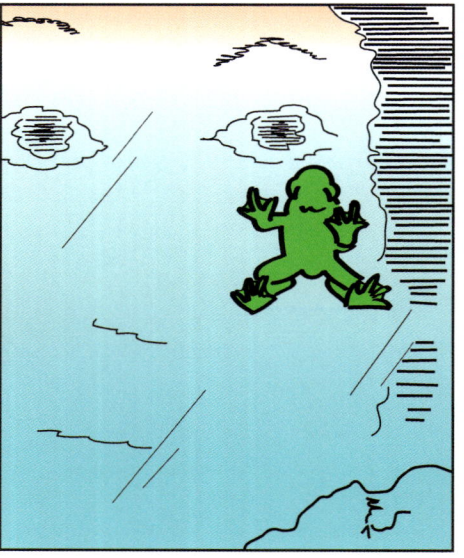

I wonder what he thinks about all day?

Lonely I'm Mister Lonely

Mister Lonely Frog

© 2002 SUZ

This will be our first time walking together in the park.

© 2001 SUE

Thank goodness, Tracer has her stopping areas ...

... and knows the way.

Go Tracer go, you four legged, furred behemoth.

Tracer Hilly Park

55

THE PETSITTER™

© 2003 SUZ

Lawn Bug Brush

The PetSitter™

Kitties live with them but never know when they'll become...

The Boogey Dog

Elvis Yarnball

The PetSitter™

I haven't seen Elvis for a bit of time...

Elvis has left the heat ducts.

Elvis Heatducts

The Bestest Times...?

Anyone who has had or who currently has a companion animal can probably relate to some or many of the adventures that I, The PetSitteR, have had with not only my companion animals, but with the many animals I have sometimes had the questionable pleasure of meeting. And as for adventures without animals, since time immemorial I believe humans have shared in these too. A comfort for the individual.

The first job I had that entailed taking care of turtles was some twenty years ago. I had forgotten about that pleasurable time with the two little terrestrial reptiles. Thank goodness I had my collection of notes, for I would not have been able to share this delightful experience with you. And if you, the clients who were the human companions to these not anonymous creatures see this book, please contact me. It would be a pleasure to chat with you again. I apologize. I do not remember your names.

Well..., Boomer and Katie the turtles, lived with not only Rusty and Chip, two canines, but also with Emma, the feline. Notice I wrote the feline, not a feline. It is not a moot point, as to whether or not cats are at the apex to the hierarchy of the bipedal and for the most part, less haired creatures in the home. The human's home is in actuality the cats. I have plenty of evidence to support this statement, but I will not at this moment.

As for Boomer and Katie, I had to watch them eat. Yes, the client ask that I watch them masticate because Boomer would eat and then, advance toward Katie's bowl to eat her food. Katie either ate too slow or would not eat at all. A wild thought that a turtle can eat slower than slow, considering the other turtle ate fast-slow or slow-fast? It is like pondering the philosophical question in Van Morrison's song lyrics, "What's the sound of one hand clapping?"

After I transported Boomer and Katie from their housing tank to their dining tank, I would place a chair next to it, sit, and watch them. Boomer was not going to over-eat while in my care. End-up looking like some form of a mobile pistachio nut due to pudgy turtle legs and a rotund, protruding belly that kept his two carapaces from closing. How would I get him to exercise away his weight? And then there was Katie to consider with her lack of a sense of time and/or appetite. To get her to eat, would Katie have known what an airplane is? "Open up Katie, here it comes, in to the hangar." Questions that only Boomer and Katie would have had the answers to.

The following entries are from the original notes on Boomer and Katie, edited to eliminate irrelevant details.

7/28 7:00 a.m.
Feeding time continues; three hours later, we are waiting for Katie to finish eating. Boomer is already back at their home base. Katie and I should go to dinner sometime. A shared attribute.

5:00 p.m.
Boomer and Katie drank some of their water but didn't eat. By the way, who forgot to tell The PetSitteR that turtles defecate in their lukewarm water? Isn't life full of learning experiences.

7/29 7:00 a.m.
Turtles not eating much. I hope this is normal behavior, that they only eat every so often.

5:00 p.m.
Turtles, I don't know. They are drinking but not eating. I gave them all the items from the list of enticing foods: cat kibble, apple, bread, and Vital-ife. They seem turtle active?

7/30 7:00 a.m.
It's fun watching the turtles not do much.

5:30 p.m.
As usual, Katie is still eating, and Boomer had me escort him back to home base.

7/31 7:30 a.m.
Anyway, all the kids have eaten but one. Guess who the One is? Rusty, Chip, and I are patiently waiting to go for our walk. Their legs are not crossed, yet.

5:30 p.m.
The turtles paid no attention to me.

10:00 p.m.
The turtles didn't acknowledge my presence. I'm hurt. No. I'm okay.

8/1 7:15 a.m.
Katie is the last to chew and chew and chew and... .

My notes ended with that entry. And I do not have any other notes from this client concerning their menagerie of punkins. (Yes, I am guilty of being anthropomorphic.) That may have been the only time that I took care of Rusty, Chip, Emma, Boomer, and Katie.

There was however, another crew of critters I had the joy of taking care of a number of times, although at times a patience tugging joy. Peter and Peggy were two Keeshonds who were supposed to kennel-up at night in their grand dog house. However, that is a story for another time. Cat was the feline who decided that after residing outdoors at a ranch during her younger years was now ready to move indoors and claim her home. Jason, a German Shorthair Pointer, usually traveled with Mom and Dad, so The PetSitteR did not have to serve his needs, and lastly, there was Charlie, the cockatiel.

Charlie. She was work, as any of you who have had or have feathered companions know. Well... some can be more chore-filled in care than others. They know how to party, as Charlie did many times. What do I mean by party?

After Peter, Peggy, and Cat were taken care of, I would go to Charlie. As I approached her abode, seeds and seed shells would crunch under my feet or pieces of fruit would squash on to the bottom of my footwear, an especially dangerous situation if I had my beloved one dollar and twenty nine cent slippery soled flip-flops on. Food and food residue would be thrown here, there, everywhere. And you know what. As soon as I returned Charlie to her spanky looking, cleaned cage with fresh food and water, her party attitude might kick-in and stuff would fly, many times while I was still within flight path range. However, it was not the food stuff that concerned me. This could be easily picked from clothing or more importantly, my hair.

While Charlie was cage free, she would hang-out on one of my shoulders and either preen my hair or just survey her Queendom. Eventually, she was returned to her cage and away I would go. One time I went, and a number of hours later, someone alerted me to the fact that I had some kind of goo on my back. Yep, it was bird goo. Amazingly, my hair had not swept through it. Charlie, Charlie, Charlie, how could I not let her continue to hang-out on my shoulders. She only did what she needed to do. Writing her name three times reminds me of the saying that, things run in threes. Bailey, Shiloh, and Fly are not things, but they were quite the threesome that ran together.

These three were definitely what I would describe as characters. When Bailey who was a greyhound looked at me, her face exuded a sweetness and an innocence. Fly, a Chow mix, and Shiloh, a large Lab mix did not evoke the same effect as Bailey, yet they were just as gentle in nature as Bailey,... when they wanted to be. Unfortunately for me, I did not get to see them when they were in their up-to-something behavior. If I had, I might have been able to salvage... . Wait, I need to make a preface here.

With every client during the initial visit, what I call the prelim visit, I try to gather as many details as possible concerning their beloved creature's physical and mental well-being, including any idiosyncrasies the animal(s) may display. It can be a time consuming process, especially when there are multiple animals to care for. Though it is well worth the information gathering time because as soon as the job begins, I am alone with them. All by my self with more times than not, teeth, nails, and swishing tails.

I had spent the night with the threesome and as usual, I had to leave that morning to see other critters, besides return to my home to check on my four-legged and furred kids. That afternoon, I pulled-up to the house to find Fly standing on the deck and I heard Shiloh and Bailey barking from inside the house. As I peered through the deck railing toward the dog door that gave the dogs access to the outdoors from the master bedroom, I saw that a pillow was lodged in the dog door frame. I realized it was my pillow, my favorite pillow. Needless to write, I rescued my pillow, which freed the other two from their confinement but you know what? That evening when I returned for the night, I found my pillow shredded with the bejesus of its insides here, there, everywhere about the bedroom. It was at that time that I realized something was missing from areas of the client's home. I had not seen one pillow; bedroom, living room, or any other pillow of sort. It was no surprise to me when later that evening, I discovered all of their pillows in a closet. Someone had forgotten to share this important detail with The PetSitteR. To this trio, as with any canine(s), a toy is a toy is a toy, unless taught otherwise.

I woke-up the next morning with an all is forgotten attitude. I have learned from the animals to live in the moment. How could I hold a grudge toward them when there was no act of spite by them. While the boys food settled in their systems, so that we could go for our morning constitution, I went to get dressed. It was just after I put-on my shorts that I realized the most important component to my attire was missing. The support for my girls, my brassière, bra, was no where to be found. Now you must understand that I am somewhat fastidious about my belongings when I go to clients homes. I keep my things in a specific area because I do not want to leave anything behind when the job is finished. This job was not finished. And I certainly would not leave my brassière?

After searching the bathroom where my shorts, teeshirt, and bra had been placed the night before, I started looking about the bedroom. Nothing, so I searched about the house. Nothing. Where the heck was my bra? I always keep my clothes together. And then, for some reason, I was drawn to one of the master bedroom windows. As I mentioned earlier, the dogs have access to the outdoors and their dog yard via a dog door in the master bedroom. After going through the door, they can either hang-out on the deck or traverse down a six foot long ramp to their yard. The yard, large in area was surrounded by a ten foot tall fence to keep predators such as mountain lions, also known as cougars at bay. Living within a mountainous area has its dangers, and most dogs are prey to these creatures.

Thank goodness when I looked-out the window, there was not a mountain lion lurking about the outer perimeter of the fence line. However, what I saw was just about as horrifying. There it was, my cherished brassière, bra in a little heap for I am not very endowed, laying in the dirt within the confines of the dog yard. I crawled through the dog door, crab walked down the ramp, and walked over to my now tattered and dirtied bra. It had been a tug toy for the terrible twosome at play, Shiloh and Fly. To them, a toy is a toy is a toy, unless taught otherwise.

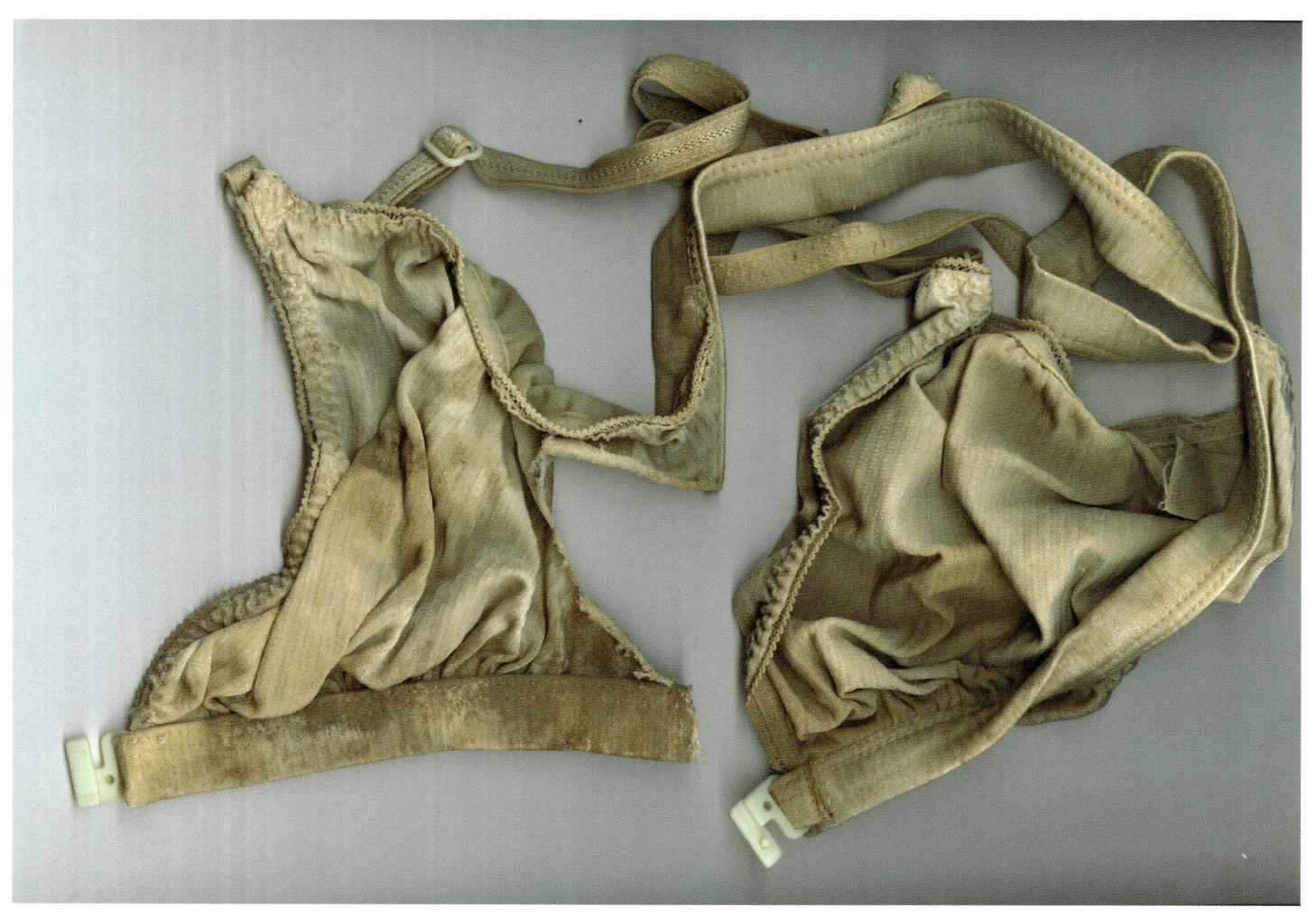

Yes folks, this is the actual brassière

It could have been as boring as boring gets to sit and watch Boomer and Katie eat, if I had taken that attitude. I did not. I relaxed and let my mind wander. As I wrote the visit notes, I enjoyed hearing the click, click, click from Charlie's talons, as she strutted about on the kitchen tabletop. Sometimes the note writing was a challenge because you know who had to peck at the stiff, yet wormlike moving object. And although seeing my treasured undergarment laying on the ground in the dog yard left me stupefied, I remember that I did chuckle. After all, at the time it was and it still is better for me, my overall well-being to react in a positive fashion than a negative one. They were just being the creatures they were born to be.

In thinking about them, as I do with all the creatures who have entered my life, the smile spreads across my face, and my soul feels euphoric.

"Beautiful memories of beautiful moments,
together."

THE PETSITTER™

WELCOME

TO

THE

POTTY

© 2001 SUZ

Buster & Cleo Bathroom Party

THE PETSITTER™

Scooter always enjoys getting his belly scratched.

Hmmmmmm. I wonder...?

That IS nice.

Happy Dog. Happy Human

© 2007 SUZ

Belly Scratchin'

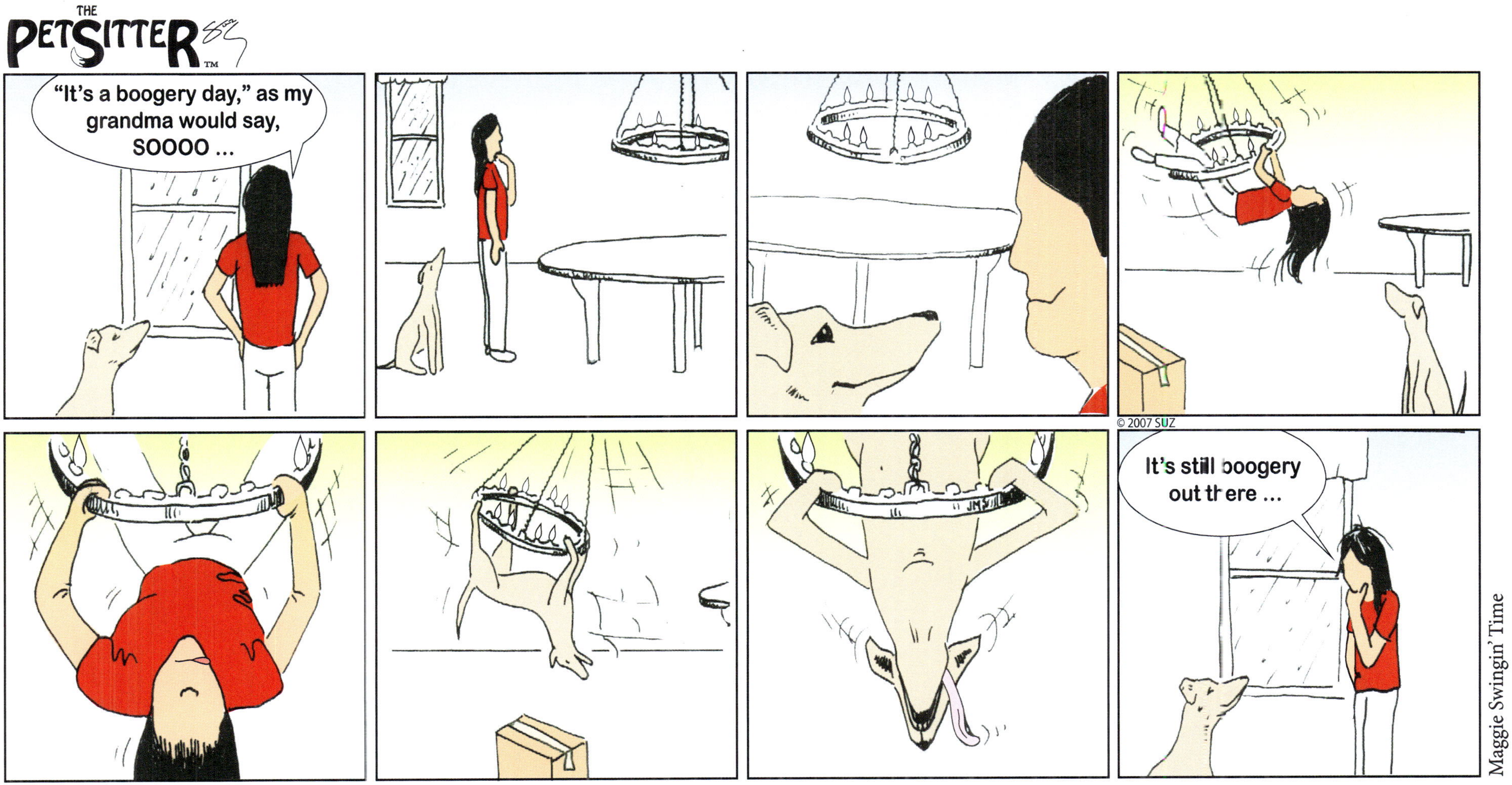

THE PETSITTER™

Just as we do, the other creatures such as Cody and Molly, need to have their senses stimulated.

But not that way.

Geesh.

Entertainment ... entertainment?

NEW!

The PetSitteR Animal Fragrance Doll

KITTY SCENT

CAT RUBBING SCENT

COW PASTURE

PETTED DOGS

MISC. FOOD SMELLS

SCENTS YOU WERE BORN WITH

HORSE SCENTS

HOURS OF FUN from SUMSCENTS4U

© 2002 SUZ

Cody The PetSitteR Doll

THE PETSITTER™

Dogs have special places they love to have scratched.

One such spot is where the fleas hang-out on Saturday night.

Welcome to the TROPICANINE

© 2001 SUZ

Saturday Night Fleas

Pandy Catnip Treats

Five's favorite toy.

Five Sparkly Balls

If you are not comfortable with the night, its darkness, perhaps you should not view these panels. If you choose to...

may you **SLEEP** well tonight?

(W) Go to sleep.

(F) I can't. She's here. I can feel her presence.

(W) Oh, you're getting old and edgy.

(F) You wait young'un. Someday you'll understand.

© 2008 SUZ

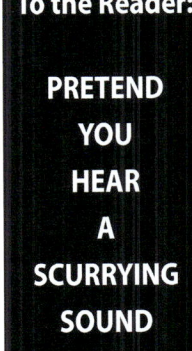

To the Reader:

PRETEND
YOU
HEAR
A
SCURRYING
SOUND

YELP!

(W) What happened?

(F) She got me.

meeeooooowwwww

STAY TOONED

Gypsy at Large

73

Gypsy, you have to stop attacking the dogs st night. Otherwise, I'll have to shut the door to keep you out of the bedroom.

I can't promise that. Besides you know your heart is too big to shut me... the cat, out of anywhere.

And you too, think it's kind of funny.

© 2008 SUZ

Gypsy at Large

74

Goddesses Of The Gull

Pandy Lotion

The PETSITTER™

As do the other creatures ...
I too rely on my keen senses.

EYES - See it. Great

NOSE - Smell it. Okay.

HANDS - Test for it.
Not so great.

FEET - Step in it. 'Nuf said.

Keen Senses

The PETSITTER™

This is Six.

I call her my
Little Paddlepuss.

Thank goodness for clumping.

Six Paddlepuss

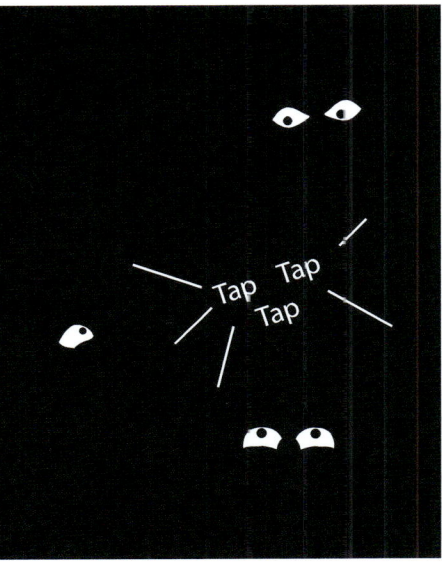

Mazy & Dakota Night Business

Three's A Crowd

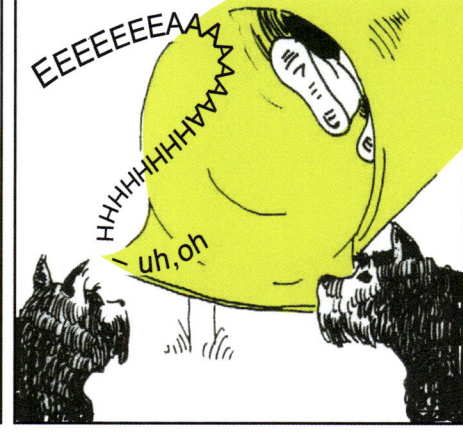

Ginger & Scooter Tube Slide

Flying Security

Our questionable habits affect them too.

81

Beyond The Physical...

I have said for many years that I plan to live to be 110 years of age and at that time, I will decide if I want to continue to live. This is part tongue-in-cheek, because I realize I may not live that long. There is one certainty though, in regards to my mortality. By living the way the other creatures do, in the moment, when my time does come to physically let go, I will feel as if I truly lived and not just survived, as I have sometimes done in the past. After all, daily living is an undulation of emotion laden events. Good, bad, happy, sad.

The dedications in this book are my way of honoring Aunt Sister, my Mother's oldest sister who passed-on in the early seventies, and my Mother who passed-on because it was her time to do so to. My Mother knew about the dedications. The words concerning my Aunt Sister's wisdom were paraphrased by me because I only had my memory of too many decades gone by to rely on. As for my Mother's part, the words are hers.

It was just about a year prior to Mom's death that we discussed what I had written for the dedications. Mom wanted one of her thoughts deleted and replaced with another. She was concerned that people might not like her because of that one thought, perhaps seen by others as an opinion, negative. I obliged her request and made the change. Too, she wanted me to finish this book while she was still alive. I did not. The Future came, as it intended to. And the Future has taken many of the animals that I have come to know, and truly care about during my pet sitting career, their life span being much shorter in duration than ours.

I remember Milo. I believe he was the first elderly canine I pet sat. Milo was smaller than usual for a Schnauzer, but even in his gettin-up-there years, he maintained that stocky frame indicative to his breed. Physical changes from the years coming and going had taken away his hearing and had left him partially blind from cataracts, but had certainly not affected his essence, as an individual and as a Schnauzer.

He never heard me enter the house, nor approach him as he laid on his bed. I was always very careful not to startle him from his deep slumber. My touch to awaken him, to alert him to my presence was gentle. I always placed my hand to the side of his face, near one of his ears. This way he would not feel threatened and possibly, bite me. Milo would look at me, and he knew what we were going to do. I hooked his leash to his collar, and out the doorway he led us.

Milo was all about taking care of his business. He walked in brisk fashion for a dog of his years, stopping to sniff the ground and then, mark specific trees or curbsides. I had to keep to his pace, not mine, for as I have written in entries to clients, I am only here to serve the animal's needs. And upon our return to the house, he would go directly to his bed, curl-up, and quickly fall asleep. When he died, I do not know. My hope is that it occurred while he was curled-up on his bed, in deep sleep. Just a little guy who will forever own a piece of me.

Brandy was a little, spaniel mix of a girl dog. Her home consisted of a family of four human companions, two kitties, and a number of horses. Brandy had entered her senior years when I started taking care of her and the other animals. Sadly, perhaps partly due to her age, she had developed congestive heart failure. At times, she would cough to clear her lungs. Yet..., it did not affect her when it came time to take our walk about the fields or interact with the horses, as I fed them.

My pet sitting visits with Brandy were suppose to be for the duration of an extended weekend trip the family was taking to visit other family members just a three hour drive away. We discussed Brandy's health issue and that her prognosis was not good. The probability of Brandy dying was quite high. And the family to a point, had resigned themselves to the reality of her pending death.

Brandy died during my care. It was a Saturday night, warm and still in weather. No moon, but plenty of stars. Brandy and I had sat next to one another on the small hill that overlooked the pasture and horses. Earlier, she had accompanied me while I took care of the horses and then, quartered the two kitties in the barn for the night, so coyotes would not have at them. We sat on the hill; me with my human thoughts and Brandy with her canine thoughts. A wonderful moment of quiet companionship. She seemed fine.

As I prepared to leave her for the night, I will never forget the feeling that came over me. In hindsight, she did not want me to leave her. This is not unusual. I find that many of the animals I have cared for and still do, at times, act as if they do not want me to leave them or perhaps more importantly, leave them alone. As we stood in the kitchen together, I looked at Brandy, told her that I loved her, and to guard the house.

That next morning, I entered the home to find Brandy dead on the floor in the exact spot where I had walked away from her. One of my little punkins, the family's canine member had passed-on sometime during the night, alone. I called another client who is a veterinarian, and asked that she please come to the home. I wanted to know if Brandy had suffered, and yes,... I felt responsible for her death. Guilt welled-up in me because I felt I had ignored my gut feeling as to something about the way she had looked at me, as I walked away from her the night before. No creature, human or animal should die alone.

The client came to the house. After she assesssed Brandy's lifeless state, she felt that Brandy did not suffer and passed-on quickly. I remember the guilt within me lessened a bit in feeling responsible for Brandy, and her subsequent death.

I placed a call to the family. Through quivering voices and tear filled eyes, we spoke to one another about Brandy. They would return home, as soon as they could get their belongings packed. They requested that Brandy's body be taken to the barn, so the other client and I wrapped her in several towels, and we took her there.

I drove home to retrieve some pieces from a large quantity of desert sage that I had collected while I lived in Arizona. I then returned to the client's home. In my final note to them, I wrote that Native Americans burn sage to bless a new dwelling, home, or a loved one. They would eventually burn the sage to bless, honor, and remember their Brandy.

If you have never had the pleasure of meeting Greyhounds, you should. If you would like a quiet, yet loyal companion who can adapt to a life of being walked while leashed to the wheelchair of his or her companion person or who with time, may tolerate the hustle and bustle of the family, you should consider adopting a Greyhound. These beautiful creatures are usually rescued after what may be a brief career as racing dogs, exploited for human entertainment and monetary gain. And sadly, there are those who are never rescued. While I lived in Arizona, a large number of racing Greyhounds no longer considered of value by some humans, were killed and their bodies were discarded in the desert; a disgusting, disrespectful act perpetrated by one creature toward another creature. I do not recall if the killers were ever caught and prosecuted. I do hope so.

Maggie was a rescued Greyhound. Simply put, a sweetheart. And unfortunately, she suffered from Colitis. Maggie had dietary constraints and she was given medication in trying to alleviate intestinal upsets that occurred from time to time. The visit I was to make with Maggie, would be our final one.

The client while away on a business trip, called me early one morning. He was flying in late that evening and his girlfriend was leaving mid morning. I was asked to make a mid-afternoon visit and possibly, an evening visit. He informed me that Maggie had been having a difficult time from the colitis. I rang his girlfriend and talked to her for an update. Earlier in the week, she had taken Maggie to the vet. She felt Maggie was doing... okay.

I arrived at the house and upon entering, I knew something was not right. Maggie did not greet me at the door. As I walked through the dining-room toward the kitchen, I saw a horrible sight. There were several pools of mucousy looking blood on the kitchen floor. I called for Maggie with no response by her.

I believe all creatures feel vulnerable, especially when their health and well-being is compromised. Depending on the circumstances, they may seek-out an isolated, quiet, and perhaps dark place for comfort and more important, safety. Because of what I had discovered in the kitchen, I felt Maggie had done just that, gone somewhere in the house other than where she would normally go. I found her in the basement. I knew I needed to get her to the vet office, as quickly as possible. Due to her physical state, I think she had gone to the basement to die.

86

There was no way by myself that I was going to get Maggie up the stairs, so I called a friend to come and help me. While I waited for Jim to arrive, I called the vet office to alert them to Maggie's condition and that I was bringing her to the office. I also called the client to let him know what had transpired with Maggie. We talked about me leaving her at the house because he was flying home. I told him I was not comfortable leaving her there at the house, in the condition I found her. Jim and I put Maggie on a blanket, as a sling, to carry her up the stairs and to my car.

Upon arriving at the vet office, several staff members assisted me in getting Maggie, still on the blanket, from my car to the critical care room. She was set-up on an I.V., for both rehydration purposes and the administration of meds. I left to carry-on to other critters. The client returned that night, late. Maggie died at the vet office that night, late, without the client being with her. Some time later he mentioned this to me, that he did not get to be with her.

There have been a few times, when thinking about my decision to take Maggie to the vet, that I have felt a bit responsible for the client not having been with Maggie, his beloved Greyhound when she passed-on. As I wrote early on in this book, I go to client's homes to care for their companion animals. I have made many a phone call to clients and to vet offices, in regard to the health and well-being of the animal(s). I live by the adage, better to be safe than sorry. I am sorry... for the way the events unfolded with Maggie and the client.

Death ended my Aunt Sister's bodily existence, as it did my Mother's, and many of the other creature's who have come in to my life. However, I believe all are still with and about me in an eternal state, as forms of energy; the spirit, the soul, two interchangeable terms. Although some believe that cell death is cell death is cell death, I look to one law of physics to justify my belief in the hereafter, Heaven. Energy can be neither created nor destroyed. The physical housing decays, yet the essence of the being, energy continues on. No more boundary by physical-ness. And I realize there is a complexity to this law and the other laws of physics that extends far beyond my knowledge base, but... death too, extends beyond anyone's knowledge base until one enters in to it.

Several times throughout the passing years, Mom and I talked about what each one wanted if decisions needed to be made in regard to our health and subsequent death. Not six months before Mom died, during one of our philosophical ponderings of a discussion, I asked her if there was any way possible after she passed-on, would she let me know that she was still with me. She said she would do just that, and whether or not you believe me, she has made her unbounded existence known to not only me a number of times, but to other family members. Too, I have sensed the presence of not only some of my companion animals who have passed-on, but the presence of client's animals after their death. During that first walk with the surviving dog(s), I have sensed what I think is the un-earthly presence of the recently deceased dog walking just behind me at my back, right side. Perhaps the walk was taken with us, to comfort us.

A few weeks before Mom died, she told me that she knew she would be with God. I now know via hindsight, by making that statement to me, that she had already begun the inner journey, letting go of her physical self and the physical world. After she died, I wrote her a letter. The letter ends,

You are our Mother, the Woman, a Woman.
Now just free-flowing energy.

And for you Mom,
"One with and of God"

Love, Suzanne

Unbounded Existence...,
No Time.
No Space.

In Memorium ...

In Memorium

This is not...

THE END